GRANDPA

GRANDPA

Lilith Norman & Noela Young

Margaret Hamilton Books

Sydney

1998

My grandfather died last Saturday.

I told all about him in class today.
  I don't often have anything to tell in class,
but today I did. It felt good.

Grandpa was a pain in the neck.

Every day, when I came home from school, he said,
'Hello, Sonny Jim, home again?'

Every day.

And every day I said, 'My name's not Sonny Jim, it's Blake.'

And then he would say, 'No grandson of mine is a Blake.
A Joe Blake. A snake!'

Then he'd snortle with laughter, and start coughing.
And he'd drop ash and bits of tobacco everywhere.
Then Mum would get mad at the mess.
Every single day.

Grandpa had worked all his life in the country
till he came to live with us. He was always
saying how soft city kids were.

Now, when he was a boy . . .

And he'd tell some boring old story about when
he was droving, or shearing, or caught in a flood.

I used to think they were terrific stories when I
was a little kid, but now I'd heard them maybe
a million times.

I won't ever hear them again.

When Grandpa came to live with us, Mum gave
him my room and I slept out in the sunroom.
It'll be good to have my own room back.

I don't think Dad liked Grandpa much. Whenever Grandpa
told one of his stories, Dad would roll his eyes at Mum and me.
    When Grandpa had finished, Dad would say, 'Good for you,
Old Timer.' He always called Grandpa 'Old Timer', the way
they do in western movies.

Grandpa always gave Dad
a dirty look then.
I think he thought Dad
was soft, too, like city kids.

When Grandpa died, Mum said, 'At least I can cook what I like now.' Then she burst into tears.

Mum used to cook terrific food before Grandpa came to live with us. Lasagne, and beef Stroganoff, and Chinese food in a wok. All that sort of stuff.

Grandpa didn't like it. 'Made up dishes,' he complained. 'That's not proper tucker.'

So mostly we had chops and roasts and sausages.

I don't know why Mum cried. You'd think she'd be pleased to be able to cook anything she liked again.

One thing Grandpa was good at was mending stuff.
When my Triple RRR Super-Zap Space Blaster busted,
he fixed it up like new.

And he made this whole shelf of little birds and animals out of horseshoe nails. Emus and kangaroos and brolgas and snakes, and an old cow scratching its head with a hoof. That was pretty clever.

And he gave them all to me.

I went to see Grandpa once when he was in hospital.
He wasn't like Grandpa at all. Just this shrunken
little old man in a bed.

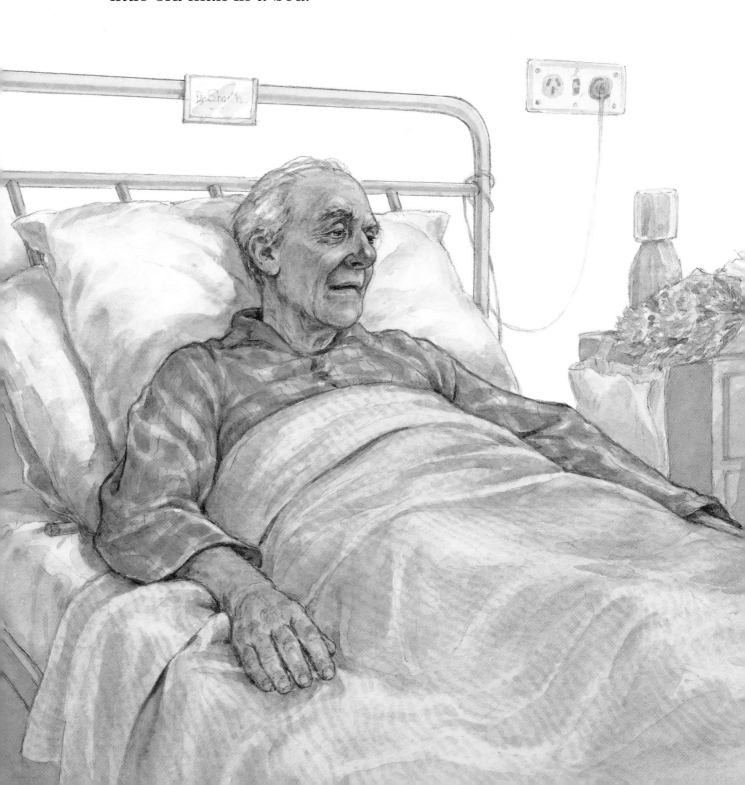

He looked at me for a long time. Then he said,
'Hello, Blake.' That's all.
   Mum said he was too sick to talk, so
we just sat there, and Mum stroked his hand.
   Then we went home.

I can remember most of the stories Grandpa used to tell. I should. I heard them often enough. But now there's no one to say, 'Hello, Sonny Jim, home again?'

Grandpa was a pain in the neck sometimes.
He was boring.
  But he could've had my room for ever.

I think I'll take his horseshoe nail animals to school tomorrow. I want to show the other kids how terrific my Grandpa was.

First published in 1998 by Margaret Hamilton Books
PO Box 28 Hunters Hill NSW 2110 Australia
A Division of Scholastic Australia Pty Limited.
© text, Lilith Norman 1998 © illustrations, Noela Young 1998
National Library of Australia Cataloguing-in-Publication entry
Norman, Lilith, 1927- . Grandpa. ISBN 0 947241 52 3.
I. Young, Noela. II. Title. A823.3.

Typeset in 17pt Baskerville
Printed in Hong Kong
9 8 7 6 5 4 3 2 1   8 9 / 9